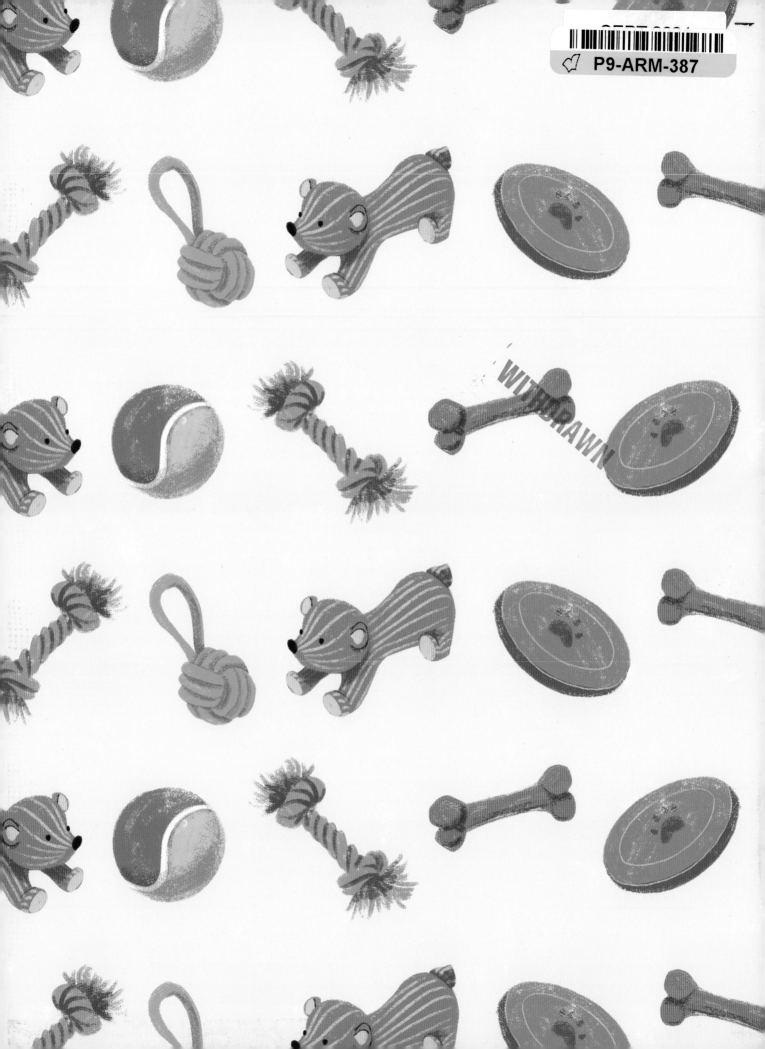

To Josh Funk, with thanks. —A. S.

To Claire Easton, thanks for believing in me. —J. S.

Henry Holt and Company, *Publishers since 1866*
Henry Holt® is a registered trademark of Macmillan Publishing Group, LLC
120 Broadway, New York, NY 10271
mackids.com

Library of Congress Cataloging-in-Publication Data
Names: Staniszewski, Anna, author. I Stone, Joanie, illustrator.
Title: Beast in show / Anna Staniszewski ; illustrated by Joanie Stone.
Description: First edition. I New York : Henry Holt and Company, 2021. I Audience: Ages 3–6.
I Audience: Grades K–1. I Summary: After Julia and her dog Huxley enter a very unusual dog
show they quickly realize the challenges of competing against fire-breathing, levitating,
extraterrestrial pets, but good-natured Huxley gives it his all.
Identifiers: LCCN 2020020576 I ISBN 9781627791267 (hardcover)
Subjects: CYAC: Dog shows—Fiction. I Monsters—Fiction. I Sportsmanship—Fiction.
Classification: LCC PZ7.S78685 Be 2021 I DDC [E]—dc23
LC record available at https://lccn.loc.gov/2020020576

Our books may be purchased in bulk for promotional, educational, or business use. Please
contact your local bookseller or the Macmillan Corporate and Premium Sales Department at
(800) 221-7945 ext. 5442 or by email at MacmillanSpecialMarkets@macmillan.com.
First edition, 2021 / Design by Liz Dresner
The art for this book was created digitally.
Printed in China by RR Donnelley Asia Printing Solutions Ltd., Dongguan City, Guangdong Province
1 3 5 7 9 10 8 6 4 2

Beast in Show

Anna Staniszewski

Illustrated by Joanie Stone

Henry Holt and Company

New York

Huxley may have seemed like an ordinary dog, but Julia knew he was a winner. She wanted everyone else to see it, too.

"Come on, Huxley," she said.

"Today is our big day."

Huxley wagged his tail hopefully.

"We can play fetch another time.

After we win the dog show!"

Julia's dad walked them over to the town hall.

But when they got inside . . .

"Is this really the dog show?"
Julia asked.

"Yup," said a judge. "Just a
totally normal dog show."

Julia stared at the other contestants. Their nails
sparkled. Their coats glistened. Their teeth gleamed.
Beside them, Huxley suddenly seemed so . . . ordinary.

Julia must have looked worried, because Huxley jumped
up and gave her nose a lick.
She smiled. "You're right, Huxley. Let's go win this thing."

First up was the obstacle course.

"Run, Huxley!"

"Jump, Huxley!"

"Do a triple backflip, Huxley!"

But Huxley couldn't compete with dogs that galloped and twirled and levitated. He was having fun, but Julia hated seeing him get lost in the crowd.

At the end of the opening round, Bob soared into first place.

"It's okay, Huxley," Julia said.
"We still have two more events."

Next the dogs were asked to speak.

"Bark, Huxley!"

"Howl, Huxley!"

"Sing 'Happy Birthday,' Huxley!"

— Arf

The other dogs beeped and breathed
fire and communicated in over a thousand
intergalactic languages.

Bob brought the crowd to tears with his magical song.

Once again, he was named the winner.

Julia groaned. The judges hadn't even looked Huxley's way!

There was only one round left.

"Come on, Huxley,"
Julia said.

"We need to get the
judges' attention. It's
time for a makeover."

After some grooming and braiding and
accessorizing, Huxley was ready.

In the final challenge, the dogs showed off their commands.

Huxley sat. He pointed. He rolled over. He did everything perfectly. But Julia could tell he was miserable.

And even after all that work, the judges still barely noticed him!

Finally, it was Bob's turn.

But as Bob went to take his place—
CRASH!

He tripped over his tail ribbon.

Everyone in the hall gasped.

Huxley didn't hesitate. He bounded
over to Bob and gave his nose a lick.

Bob pulled himself together.

With Huxley at his side, he finished the competition.

At the end, Bob posed like a champion.
Huxley stood proudly beside him.
    The crowd cheered. Julia even heard
people chanting Huxley's name!
    "Good boy, Huxley!" Julia said.

As the judges prepared to announce the winner, Julia held her breath.

"We have reached a decision!" the judges said. "This year's Best in Show is . . .

"...Bob!"

Julia couldn't believe it. Huxley had done
everything right, and he still didn't win!

She pulled out Huxley's hair clips and
bows and braids until he was himself again.
Julia must have looked upset, because
Huxley jumped up and gave her nose a lick.
"All right, Huxley," Julia said, rubbing
his ears. "We'll try again next year."

Suddenly, Bob trotted over, scooped Huxley up, and paraded him around the Winner's Circle. Julia had never seen Huxley look so happy! The crowd erupted in applause. Julia joined in. Huxley might have been a winner, but Bob deserved to be Best in Show.

When Huxley was on the ground again, he ran over to Julia with part of Bob's prize.

Huxley wagged his tail hopefully.

Julia smiled. "Good idea, Huxley," she said. "Let's go play fetch."

WANT TO MAKE YOUR DOG "BEST IN SHOW"?
TRY TEACHING YOUR PET THESE FIVE EASY COMMANDS!
(You may need a grown-up's help.)

Sit

Hold a treat above your dog's nose and then lift the treat above their head and say, "Sit." Repeat until your dog's bottom touches the ground and then reward your dog with a treat.
Bonus: If your dog has wings, you can try this in a tree!

Come

Walk a few feet away from your dog and then call your dog's name and say, "Come!" in an excited tone. When your dog comes to you, reward them with praise or a treat.
Note: If your dog is in outer space, you may need to call them using a satellite dish.

Spin Around

Hold a treat above your dog's nose and spin it in a slow circle. Encourage your dog to follow the treat with their nose, until they spin around. Reward with a treat. Then add the command "Spin around." Caution: If your dog can breathe fire, watch out for your fingers!

Find It

Hide a treat in plain sight and tell your dog to "Find it." Then try hiding the treat farther away or out of sight and enjoy watching your dog sniff it out. Fun Fact: Pets with X-ray vision can find almost anything!

Fetch

Have your dog "Sit" and then toss a toy in front of them and say, "Fetch." When your dog picks up the toy in their mouth, ask them to "Come" and reward with a treat. Put the toy farther away and repeat. Tip: Is your dog a real winner? Try this with a Frisbee!